W9-AAH-972

A Hero Named Howe

by **Mike Leonetti**

illustrations by
Greg Banning

RAINCOAST BOOKS

Vancouver

Text copyright © 2006 by Mike Leonetti
Illustrations copyright © 2006 by Greg Banning

All rights reserved. Raincoast Books is a member of Access Copyright. No part of this publication may be reproduced, stored in a retrieval system or transmitted in any form or by any means without prior written permission from the publisher or a license from Access Copyright. For a copyright license, visit www.accesscopyright.ca or call toll-free 1-800-893-5777.

Raincoast Books gratefully acknowledges the ongoing support of the Canada Council for the Arts, the British Columbia Arts Council and the Government of Canada through the Book Publishing Industry Development Program (BPIDP).

Cover and interior design by Teresa Bubela

Library and Archives Canada Cataloguing in Publication
Leonetti, Mike, 1958-
        A hero named Howe / Mike Leonetti ; illustrations by Greg Banning.
ISBN 10 1-55192-931-7
ISBN 13 978-1-55192-931-6
        1. Howe, Gordie, 1928—-Juvenile fiction.   2. Hewitt, Foster, 1902-1985—Juvenile
fiction.   3. Detroit Red Wings (Hockey team)—-Juvenile fiction.   I. Banning, Greg
II. Title.
PS8573.E58734H47 2006   jC813'.54   C2006-901523-6

Library of Congress Control Number: 2006923725

Raincoast Books   *In the United States:*
9050 Shaughnessy Street   Publishers Group West
Vancouver, British Columbia   1700 Fourth Street
Canada V6P 6E5   Berkeley, California
www.raincoast.com   94710

Printed in China.

10 9 8 7 6 5 4 3 2 1

ACKNOWLEDGEMENTS
The author consulted the following reference material:
Books by these authors: Kevin Allen, Stan Fischler, Colleen Howe, Gordie Howe, Roy McSkimming, Don O'Reilly, Frank Orr, Andrew Podnieks and Jim Vipond.
Reference Books: *NHL Guide and Record Book*, *Total Hockey*, Detroit Red Wings media guides.
Magazines: *Hockey News*, *Hockey Illustrated*, *Hockey Pictorial*, *Maclean's*, and Detroit Red Wings game program from 1963-64 season.
Newspaper: *Globe and Mail*.
Video/Films: *Greatest Sports Legends* and *ESPN Sports Century*.
The author would like to thank Hockey Hall of Fame broadcaster Chuck Kaiton for sharing his memories and to Fan 590 Radio in Toronto for the use of their interview with Mr. Kaiton.

This book is dedicated to Gordie and Colleen Howe and their entire family.

— Mike Leonetti

To all of our heroes — past, present and future.

— Greg Banning

It was a hot day in August but my mind was on **ice hockey**. Dad was driving me to the Detroit Olympia for the Detroit Red Wings hockey school. I was excited about meeting the players who were going to be my instructors. Best of all, my hero **Gordie Howe** was going to be there!

Gordie Howe was the **best player** in the National Hockey League. He won the most valuable player award last year when he had 49 goals and 46 assists, and he led the league in points. Howe was named to the first all-star team and he led the Red Wings to the finals, but the Toronto Maple Leafs beat them for the Stanley Cup.

Gordie was a **big, strong player** and he was fast and graceful on his skates. Few players could catch him. He had a powerful snap shot and it seemed like he could score anytime he wanted. Next season he was going for the record for most goals and he needed just **five more** to break the great Rocket Richard's mark!

I collected all of Gordie Howe's hockey cards. I couldn't wait for the 1963-64 set so that I could get Gordie's **first!** I had a Red Wings calendar in my room and Howe's picture was on the first page. I hoped the Red Wings would make it to the finals again this year.

At the hockey school we dressed quickly and skated onto the ice. We warmed up until the Red Wing players came out. I recognized Terry Sawchuk, Alex Delvecchio, Bill Gadsby and Marcel Pronovost, and then I saw him – Gordie Howe! He looked so big in his bright red sweater with **number nine** on the back. We were in awe. I was in the group that was going to be taught by Gordie! **What luck!**

Gordie told us that we should practice all types of shots — he showed us the snap shot, the backhand, the wrist shot and the slap shot. He said we should keep the goalie **guessing** about which shot we were going to use. I listened carefully and practiced the way Gordie showed us.

Before our day was finished we played a game with the Red Wing players. I was on Gordie's team! When Gordie had the puck **nobody** could take it from him. It was as if the puck was glued to his stick. I saw him stick-handling up the ice and I skated hard, hoping to catch up. I got into the open, and Gordie quickly passed the puck to me. The goalie and I were both so surprised that I had almost the whole net to shoot at, but I missed it **completely!**

After the game, Gordie skated over to me. "What's your name, son?" he asked.

"Charles, sir, but everyone calls me Charlie," I replied, trying hard not to shake.

Gordie smiled, which made me feel better, and said, "Charlie, I did all that work to set you up and you missed the net. **How come?"**

"I guess I'm just not that good," I said weakly.

"That's not true, Charlie. I surprised you with that pass. You'll get better if you practice hard. Try holding your stick like this," Gordie said, as he showed me where to place my hands. "Always **have fun** playing hockey, and do your best. Let's talk more tomorrow."

The week **flew** by. I enjoyed the Red Wings hockey school and learned many things from Gordie Howe and the others. Summer was over and it was time for regular school. Soon the Red Wings' season would begin and I wondered **how long** it would take Gordie to set the new record. He needed five goals! I followed Detroit's games on my transistor radio, listening to Budd Lynch doing the play-by-play on WWJ Radio 950. I loved the colourful way he described the action.

On Sunday nights Dad would let me listen to **Foster Hewitt** calling games on CBC Radio. Hewitt got excited at just the right moments! On Saturday nights Dad and I would watch "Hockey Night in Canada" on channel nine.

I followed **every** Red Wings' game, hoping Gordie would get the record! In his first game, Gordie scored two goals when Detroit beat Chicago. He scored **another** goal against the Boston Bruins but then went four games without scoring. Finally, he scored a goal against the Montreal Canadiens to tie the record, but then another five games went by and Gordie just couldn't score. He was **stuck** at 544!

While Gordie Howe was trying to set a new record, I started playing in the Detroit Parks and Recreation League. I was improving but often had a hard time keeping up with the play. I was a good skater but hockey moves **so quickly!** I often felt lost on the ice and my shot was a bit weak. My coach was trying to help but I wasn't nearly as good as my teammates or as Mark Howe, Gordie's son who played in the same league. I was discouraged but I **kept practicing** like Gordie told me to.

I felt better in November, on my **birthday**. Mom bought me a book written by **Gordie Howe!** The title was *Hockey ... Here's Howe* and the cover had a drawing of Gordie and his two sons. My favourite uncle gave me Gordie's newest hockey card. But the best gift of all was from Dad — **two tickets to a Red Wings game!** The tickets said GAME 8, Sunday, November 10, 1963, Detroit Red Wings vs. Montreal Canadiens.

"Hey Dad! Maybe we'll see Gordie break the record," I said, hardly believing I was going to see my first NHL game at the Olympia!

That night I stayed up late reading Gordie's book. He explained how he thought hockey should be played, and I learned many new things about the game. Gordie said you had to be dedicated to hockey **all year long** and that you had to work well with your teammates. He also said not to ignore things outside of hockey, like family and schoolwork. But the most interesting thing Gordie said was that even though **everyone** who plays hockey wants to make it to the NHL, few are good enough to do it. He said you could find other ways to help your favourite team, and that there were many jobs in hockey **besides** being a player.

"That's interesting," I thought, before drifting off to sleep.

The next day was Saturday. I had fun at my game and played my best, and I **finally** scored a goal! My coach was happy.

At dinner that night I talked to Mom and Dad about what I read in Gordie Howe's book.

"I wish I could be a great player and make it to the NHL," I explained, "but **maybe** I can do something else if I can't be a professional player."

"Is there something you would like to try, Charlie?" Mom asked.

"Well, I like listening to broadcasters like Foster Hewitt. I might try that," I replied, trying to sound confident.

"That's a good idea," Dad said. "You're good at paying attention to plays."

Then **Dad** had a good idea.

"Why don't you do the play-by-play during the game tomorrow night?" Dad said. "It'll be a good opportunity to see if you can **keep up** with the action."

"I can try," I said nervously.

The next night we left early for the Olympia. I could smell the hotdogs and popcorn when we walked in. We bought snacks and a program, and I got a Gordie Howe pennant and photograph. We were looking at a large picture in the lobby, of Gordie scoring a goal against Johnny Bower of Toronto. My Dad noticed Foster Hewitt standing nearby — he was at the Olympia to broadcast the game! We started chatting with him.

"Do you think Howe will set the record this evening?" he asked.

"I hope so, Mr. Hewitt," I said. "This might be the only game I see this year so I hope he gets the goal tonight.".

"Mr. Hewitt, my son is interested in being a **hockey broadcaster**," Dad said. "Do you have any advice?"

Foster Hewitt smiled. "Well, you have to be clear and accurate, especially when you are on radio," he replied. "And make sure you know all the players in the league, and pay close attention to which players are on the ice. It's a great job, son — good luck!" **He waved** and went to prepare for the game.

Dad and I went to our seats in section 21 in the balcony, near centre ice. We had the first two seats in the **last row!** Over 15,000 people were crammed into the Olympia to see Detroit and Montreal.

There was no scoring in the first period. The Red Wings finally got the first goal when Bruce MacGregor scored early in the second period. Five minutes later, Alex Faulkner scored to make it 2-0 for Detroit. For the next ten minutes there was no scoring. Then Faulkner got a five-minute penalty for high-sticking and it looked like Montreal had a chance to get into the game.

"Hey Charlie, here's a good chance to do a play-by-play, with Montreal on the power-play," Dad suggested. "The Red Wings will try to kill the penalty so you won't have to worry about them scoring. Give it a try. **Let's hear you do it.**"

"Okay Dad. Give me a minute to see who's on the ice," I said, remembering Foster Hewitt's advice.

I scanned the players, and a few seconds later I started my play-by-play.

"Jean Beliveau of the Canadiens shoots the puck around the boards in the Detroit end. Pronovost picks up the loose puck and gives it to Howe. Howe passes to Billy McNeill and the Wings start on a rush with Gadsby joining the attack. Three Canadiens are trapped in the Detroit end! Only Beliveau and Jacques Laperriere are back for Montreal."

I was so excited it was **hard to continue!**

"McNeill moves to the middle, fakes a pass to Gadsby and gives it to Howe. Howe snaps a shot. **HE SCORES! Gordie Howe has broken the NHL all-time scoring record!** He beat Charlie Hodge in the Montreal net! Howe is leaping for joy behind the Montreal net and his teammates are mobbing him."

"Charlie, that was great!" Dad said.

"Not bad, kid!" said a man standing behind us.

"Thanks," I said. "That was **perfect timing**. My first ever play-by-play was a record-breaking goal by my hero Gordie Howe!"

The crowd gave Gordie a standing ovation and they stopped the game for more than ten minutes. Jean Beliveau went over to shake Gordie's hand.

The Red Wings won the game 3-0.

After the game Dad took me to the door where the players come out. Soon Gordie arrived and was swarmed by people who wanted his autograph. He was patient and signed for **everybody**.

When it was my turn he said, "I remember you. You're Charlie, from the hockey school."

Yes sir," I said. "I read your book and I've decided that if I don't make the NHL I'll try something else to stay with hockey, just like you wrote. Maybe I'll be a broadcaster like Foster Hewitt."

"That's a good idea. There are **many ways** to contribute. You might have a gift for being a broadcaster, but you'll have to work at it if you want to be as good as Foster Hewitt."

"That's right," said Foster Hewitt, who had just walked through the doors. "Keep practicing, and keep enjoying the game."

I smiled at two hockey legends.

On the way home I looked at the photo of Gordie, with his signature: "To Charlie, Good Luck from Gordie Howe." I would always treasure it. And I got Foster Hewitt's signature on my program.

Dad said, "Gordie Howe and Foster Hewitt are great hockey people, Charlie. If you keep practicing, you might go far playing hockey. But if you don't get to play with the pros, maybe you can be a broadcaster."

"That would be great. Doing the play-by-play was fun, and I'll never forget describing Gordie Howe's record goal. I got good advice from Foster Hewitt. If I work at it, I could be good at broadcasting, thanks to Gordie Howe and what he wrote in his book. He's a hero in every way."

To Charlie,
Good Luck From
Gordie Howe

About Gordie Howe

Gordie Howe was born on March 31, 1928 in Floral, Saskatchewan. He joined the Red Wings in 1946 and won four Stanley Cups with Detroit. Howe led the NHL in points six times in his career and won the Hart Trophy as the league's best player six times. He was the first player to record 1,000 career points and was selected to the NHL all-star team a record 21 times. His highest single-season point total came in 1968-69 when he recorded 103 (44 goals, 59 assists). Howe's career totals include 801 NHL goals (second only to Wayne Gretzky), 1,049 assists and 1,850 points. He holds the NHL record for most seasons played (26) and for most consecutive 20 or more goal seasons (22). He retired from the Red Wings in 1971 but came back to play in the World Hockey Association in 1973-74; he was named the WHA's most valuable player. Gordie Howe played one last NHL season as a Hartford Whaler in 1979-80 when he was 52 years old.

About Foster Hewitt

Foster Hewitt was born on November 21, 1902 in Toronto. He attended the University of Toronto where he was an intercollegiate boxing champion. On March 22, 1923 Hewitt completed one of the very first hockey broadcasts from the Mutual Street Arena in Toronto. Soon he became famous doing broadcasts of Toronto Maple Leaf games on radio (and later television) and for his familiar opening: "Hello Canada and hockey fans here and in the United States!" Hewitt developed the art of hockey play-by-play as he excitedly described games to millions of fans across Canada and the northern United States. He was known for his famous goal call, "He shoots, he scores!" and was better known than some of the players! He was a successful businessman and opened a radio station in 1951 with call letters bearing his name (CKFH). Hewitt was the TV broadcaster for the famous 1972 Canada-Russia series. He retired in 1981 and died in 1985. He is a member of the Hockey Hall of Fame as a builder (elected in 1965).